Dedicated to Rachael Eidem.
Thank you for planting the seed.

www.mascotbooks.com

Ian-John and the Leprechaun

For more information, please contact:
Mascot Books
560 Herndon Parkway #120
Herndon, VA 20170
info@mascotbooks.com

Library of Congress Control Number: 2016910180

CPSIA Code: PRT0716A
ISBN: 978-1-63177-613-7

Printed in the United States

Ian-John
and the
Leprechaun

Fran Spencer & Sean Patrick Spencer

art by Cheryl Crouthamel

A long time ago in the beautiful town of Ballyshannon, Ireland, a boy named Ian-John McManus lived with his mom and sister, Mary Alice. He was a lad of ten on that sunny day in July when his whole life changed.

Part of his many chores included taking care of the sheep with his dog, Jackie-Boy. Every day in the late afternoon, Ian-John and Jackie-Boy had to gather the sheep for the night.

There was always one wandering beyond the field that gave him trouble, and she was missing again. Ian-John knew Jackie-Boy would have to find her, but poor Jackie-Boy was getting old. He couldn't run like he used to and his hearing was bad. The two walked through the fields and over the hills but couldn't catch a glimpse of the sheep.

He was afraid they would have to go into the forest where his mom told him never to go! It was getting darker, but he didn't dare return without the missing sheep.

They walked and walked until they started to tire. Ian-John decided to rest on a big rock as the wind picked up. He could hear leaves rustling and thought he finally found the missing sheep! Ian-John turned to look for the sheep but felt the strangest thing.

He felt something pinching the back of his neck. He heard laughter and all of a sudden, a little man dressed in a sparkly green outfit stood before him! As Ian-John stared, the little man said, "Don't be lookin' at me like I got two heads, boy. Haven't you ever seen a leprechaun before?"

"My name is Sean-Patrick Shaunessey, at your service. I know where your precious little sheep is, and me lips are sealed!" He then disappeared into the forest.

Ian-John knew he had no choice but to spend the night, so he found a clearing between some bushes and decided to stay there with Jackie-Boy.

In the morning, Ian-John decided to wash his face and look for the sheep again. When he finished, he could hear talking just over the hill. He and Jackie-Boy snuck up quietly.

At the top of the hill,
he saw a little house.

Sean-Patrick stood in front of the tiny door, and Ian-John heard him sing, "Shakin' me finger, shakin' me toe. You'll never find me wherever you go!"

The door then magically opened, and Ian-John knew that must be where the leprechaun was hiding the sheep.

Ian-John sang the same magic song as the leprechaun, and the door opened. The leprechaun was holding his sheep!

As soon as their eyes met, Sean-Patrick bolted out the back door, and Ian-John chased after him! They ran up the hill, down the hill, up the hill, and down again.

Then Ian-John saw Sean-Patrick disappear into a cave and followed him. He saw hanging bottles, potions, and mysterious bags.

When Sean-Patrick realized Ian-John was behind him, he grabbed one of the magic bottles and smashed it on the cave floor.

The floor opened into a huge portal, and Sean-Patrick jumped in, with Ian-John and Jackie-Boy following close behind.

When Ian-John emerged, he was just outside the fence at home. He walked slowly to tell his mother and Mary Alice the bad news.

But Ian-John didn't realize Sean-Patrick
was watching him from nearby.

Ian-John had a feeling he would never see the sheep again.

They were happy to see him but were very disappointed when Ian-John told them about the stolen sheep.

When Ian-John went to bed that night, he kept thinking about the leprechaun and his tricks.

The leprechaun's song played over in his head, *Shakin' me finger, shakin' me toe. You'll never find me wherever you go.*

He finally drifted off to sleep. And before he knew it, the morning sun was peeking through the window.

While he was having his tea and biscuit, he heard a thump at the door. Ian-John sprang to his feet. The lost sheep had been returned!

Around the sheep's neck there was a little pouch with three shiny gold coins and a note.

The note said, "Thought I could fool ya, but I knew from the start, you chased me and chased me 'til you touched me heart."

Ian-John knew the leprechaun wasn't bad, and with the three coins, he was able to buy a cow for the family.

With a warm feeling in his heart, Ian-John knew he had a new friend for life in Sean-Patrick Shaunessey.

About the Author

Fran Spencer and her grandson, Sean Patrick, enjoy using their imaginations in their writing. Ireland is a fascinating subject for both of them. Sean Patrick has always expressed a desire to explore his strong Irish heritage and connect with the magic of Ireland.

Have a book idea?

Contact us at:

Mascot Books
560 Herndon Parkway
Suite 120
Herndon, VA 20170

info@mascotbooks.com | www.mascotbooks.com